This **Picture Mammoth** *belongs to*

_____

_____

For Tom

Tom's Rainbow Walk

Catherine Anholt

"Have a little rest now, Tom," said Granny,
"and while you're asleep I'm going to knit you
a lovely new sweater."

"What colour would you like?"
"Red, please," said Tom, "or green.
But I like blue too and yellow . . ."

Before Tom had chosen a colour,
he was fast asleep and dreaming . . .

He was chasing an enormous ball of wool
down the steps into Granny's garden.

The wool rolled right up to the pond
where two foxes sat fishing.
"Hello," said Tom. "Can you help me
to choose a colour for my new sweater?"
"Of course," said the foxes. "Red is the best
colour, like our fur coats."
"Thank you," said Tom, "I think I'd like
a red sweater."

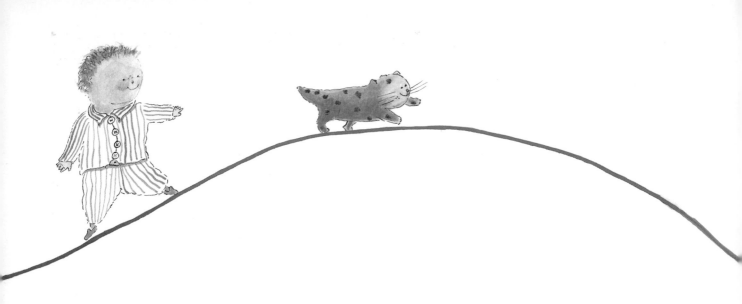

Tom ran on until he found some
little chicks playing in the yard.
"Hey, chicks," he called.
"What colour do *you* think my
new sweater should be?"
"We like yellow," they cheeped.
"Maybe they're right," thought Tom.
"I do like their fluffy yellow feathers."

At the far end of the pond
a family of frogs were hopping about.
"What 's your favourite colour, frogs?" called Tom.
"Green, green, green," they croaked.
"I like green, too," said Tom.

Just then a big blue fish
popped out of the water.

"If you're looking for a colour
and you don't know what to do,
choose any colour of the rainbow,
as long as it is blue," he called.
"That's it," said Tom,
"blue is a good colour for a sweater."

Tom skipped down to the vegetable patch
where a large pink pig
was sitting in a wheelbarrow
eating grapes.
"What colour should my new sweater be?"
called Tom.
"Try purple like these juicy grapes,
or pink," chomped the pig.
"Yes, I think pink."
"You're right," said Tom. "Pink is best."

Before he knew it, Tom had walked
all round Granny's garden
and back to the house.
A cockerel was perched on the window ledge.

"Cock-a-doodle-do," he crowed,
"I'll tell you what to do.
Choose *all* the colours of the rainbow,
not just one or two."

Tom climbed in through the window
and was just about to jump
down onto the floor when he woke up.
"Of course," he shouted.
"I'd like a rainbow sweater."

And there was Granny just finishing his sweater.
It was red as a fox,
yellow as a chick,
green as a frog,
blue as a fish,
pink as a pig
and as colourful as a cockerel.
And it fitted perfectly.

First published in Great Britain 1989
by William Heinemann Ltd
Published 1993 by Mammoth
an imprint of Reed International Books Ltd.
Michelin House, 81 Fulham Road, London SW3 6RB

10 9 8 7 6 5 4 3 2

Copyright © Catherine Anholt 1989

ISBN 0 7497 0566 3

A CIP catalogue record for this title is available from the British Library

Printed in the U.A.E. by Oriental Press Ltd.